Escape to
California

FLAT STANLEY's
WORLDWIDE ADVENTURES (12)
BOOK No

Escape to
California

CREATED BY **Jeff Brown**
WRITTEN BY **Josh Greenhut**
PICTURES BY **Macky Pamintuan**

HARPER
An Imprint of HarperCollinsPublishers

Flat Stanley's Worldwide Adventures #12: Escape to California
Text copyright © 2014 by the Trust u/w/o Richard C. Brown a/k/a Jeff Brown f/b/o
Duncan Brown.
Illustrations by Macky Pamintuan, copyright © 2014 by HarperCollins Publishers.
All rights reserved. Printed in the United States of America.
No part of this book may be used or reproduced in any manner whatsoever without
written permission except in the case of brief quotations embodied in critical articles
and reviews. For information address HarperCollins Children's Books, a division of
HarperCollins Publishers, 195 Broadway, New York, NY 10007.
www.harpercollinschildrens.com

Library of Congress catalog card number: 2014942408
ISBN 978-0-06-218991-2 (trade bdg.) — ISBN 978-0-06-218990-5 (pbk.)

Typography by Alison Klapthor
14   15   16   17   18   CG/RRDC   10 9 8 7 6 5 4 3 2 1
❖
First Edition

For the Real Lily

CONTENTS

1

Caught in San Francisco

The hills in San Francisco were so steep that all the parked cars looked as if they were going to roll away. Stanley Lambchop was climbing the sidewalk alongside his old friend Thomas Anthony Jeffrey, whom the Lambchops were visiting on their family vacation.

"I can't believe how much has happened since the last time I saw you,"

Stanley said to Thomas as they walked with Stanley's parents and brother, Arthur, up the hill. "You had just moved to California, and it was my first time traveling by mail. I hadn't even been flat long enough to get creased!"

Thomas laughed. "I remember opening your envelope. You smelled like egg salad."

Arthur shook his head. "I told you, Mom: Egg salad and milk in the mail is a bad idea!"

"*Are* a bad idea," corrected Stanley's mother, who was a stickler for good grammar. "I didn't want Stanley to go hungry. After all, it was his first time away from home!"

"I remember thinking, *California, wow!*" Stanley went on. "I'd never traveled so far away. And to think, now I've been all over the world."

"You have had a lot of excitement," said Thomas. Then he added playfully, "Though you still kind of smell like egg salad."

"I do not!" cried Stanley, cracking up.

Since the bulletin board over Stanley's bed had fallen and flattened him, he had been to Egypt, Kenya, France, Australia, and lots of other places—but there was still something nice about exploring a city like San Francisco with his family and a good friend. Thomas had shown them Haight-

Ashbury, where everyone seemed to be wearing tie-dye T-shirts, and taken them on an old-fashioned-looking cable car to Union Square, where people in business suits hurried in and out of skyscrapers. Except for the moment at Fisherman's Wharf when a group of tourists had recognized Stanley and insisted on taking pictures with him, Stanley felt like a regular sightseer. Now they were heading to the Japantown district for dinner.

As they came to the top of the hill, Stanley suddenly heard a scream. He spun around to see a girl in a wheelchair barreling down the middle of the street.

"HELP!" the girl shrieked.

Stanley leaped into action. "Thomas, throw me! Quick!"

"What?" said Thomas, in shock.

But then Arthur stepped up, took Stanley's hands, and launched him into the air like a boomerang.

"Stanley, don't!" his father yelled after him. As the wheelchair zoomed past, Stanley caught the back of it with both arms. His body ballooned backward like a parachute, and the wheelchair slowed.

"I have you!" Stanley reassured the girl.

But then he felt a tug at his back. His father had caught up and grabbed Stanley's shirt.

"Stanley!" Mr. Lambchop gasped. "It's not safe!"

"Dad! Let go!" yelled Stanley. "I have this under control!"

With his father pulling on him, one of Stanley's hands came loose from the back of the wheelchair, and his body swung backward.

"Eek!" screeched Mr. Lambchop. Now they were all in trouble. It was as if Mr. Lambchop were hang gliding behind the speeding wheelchair—and Stanley was the glider.

Now it was Stanley and his father's turn to scream, "HELP!"

Suddenly, the wheelchair came to a halt. Stanley shot over the girl's head, and his father went flying after him.

They landed with a thunk in the open bay of a cargo van, which was parked at the bottom of the hill. The girl rolled up a ramp into the van after them. She appeared to be in perfect control.

"Let's blow this taco stand!" she called to the driver.

Suddenly the doors swung closed, and the van peeled away.

The Redwood Forest

Stanley sat up. The back of the van was bare, except for a complicated-looking set of instruments and television screens on one wall. There were no windows—just a slit at the front, through which Stanley could make out the back of the driver's head.

"My name is Lily Fox," said the girl in the wheelchair. "It's an honor to

meet you, Mr. Lambchop. You're a hero
of mine."

"What? Oh, uh, thank you," stammered Stanley's father.

"Actually, I was talking to Stanley," said Lily.

All at once, Stanley realized what was happening. "You're kidnapping me!" he blurted. "Just like my friend Oda Nobu's fans kidnapped him when I was in Japan!"

Mr. Lambchop pointed a finger at Lily Fox. "How dare you! Don't you know it's impolite to kidnap people?"

"We're not kidnapping you," Lily answered calmly. "You don't have to come with us if you don't want to."

For the first time, Stanley noticed the wheels on the girl's wheelchair. They were big, studded, and rugged, like a mountain bike's tires.

Stanley got to his feet. "What do you want?"

Lily Fox wheeled over to the console and pushed some buttons. A grainy black-and-white video flickered to life on one of the screens: It was a street scene with a crowd of people. A boy walked up to a cardboard cutout and shook it roughly.

Wait a minute, thought Stanley. *That's me and that boy at Fisherman's Wharf earlier today!*

Stanley's stomach turned as he remembered the kid's face. The boy had recognized Stanley as "the famous flat kid." Without even asking, he had pulled Stanley's head back and put his chin on Stanley's shoulders so it looked as though his head was perched atop a flat body. "Quick! Take a picture!" He'd cackled to a friend. Stanley had been too embarrassed to speak. He might as well have been a painted wooden character at a carnival.

"Stanley, do you ever get tired of people looking at you funny?" asked Lily, bringing him back to the present.

Stanley sucked in his breath. "Sometimes," he said.

On the screen, his head was tucked out of sight as people crowded around and started lining up to have their pictures taken.

"Do you ever feel as if you're invisible? Like all that most people can see is that you're different, and they can't see anything else?"

On the screen, Mr. Lambchop shooed everyone away with an angry wag of his finger. In the van, he gently squeezed Stanley's shoulder.

Stanley looked at his feet. "Yeah. I guess."

The girl pushed a button, and the screen went black. "Then imagine what it's like being in a wheelchair."

Stanley looked at Lily for what felt like the first time. She was a few years older than he was. Her hair was pulled back in a dark ponytail. She looked athletic, and there was something strong about her face. She looked . . . determined.

With a slight jolt, the van came to a stop. A moment later the driver opened the cargo doors. He was a tall man wearing a tank top, Bermuda shorts, and flip-flops.

"Welcome to the Muir Woods," said the man. "I'm Theo Fox, Lily's father."

"Mr. Fox," said Stanley's dad, "I think you and Lily have some explaining to do."

"It's Dr. Fox," the man corrected.

"And that's why we're here."

Stanley looked around. They were in the middle of a forest . . . except the trees were so much larger than any Stanley had ever seen. Some seemed as big as skyscrapers.

"These are the redwoods, or Sequoias," said Dr. Fox. "They're among the biggest, oldest trees on Earth. We Foxes always come here when we have a big decision to make."

"Amazing," Stanley whispered, gazing up at the trees.

"Stanley, you said yourself that you're tired of others judging you by your appearance. I feel the same way. And I think it's time to change how the

world sees people in wheelchairs."

Stanley nodded. He knew what she meant. "But how?"

"By pulling off one of the greatest stunts of all time," Lily answered matter-of-factly. "I'm going to escape from Alcatraz, without the use of my legs, on live TV."

"Alcatraz!" said Mr. Lambchop. "The old prison? Nobody has ever successfully escaped from there! I read about it in my guidebook. It's perched on a rocky island in the middle of San Francisco Bay, surrounded by shark-infested waters! They call it the Rock."

"The one and only," said Lily.

Mr. Lambchop shook his head. "But

it's impossible—"

"You might be surprised by what I can do in my wheelchair," interrupted Lily. "That's the whole point!"

With that, Lily shot forward, her hands spinning both wheels so quickly, they were a blur. Dirt and leaves sprayed behind her. She curved sideways up the base of a giant redwood, and then rolled up the base of another, as if she were moving between a pair of skateboard ramps. Finally she lifted herself out of her wheelchair, spun the chair around, and sat again.

She came to stop in front of them, with one eyebrow raised as if to say, *See?*

"That was incredible!" Stanley cried, clapping. But then he shook his head. "I still don't understand how *I* can help *you.*"

Lily wheeled up close. "Is it true that you found your way out of a pyramid in Egypt? That you trained with Oda Nobu in Japan and performed with the

Flying Chinese Wonders in Beijing?"

Stanley nodded.

"Then help me pull off the greatest escape ever," said Lily.

Stanley's heart skipped a beat. His eyes climbed the majestic trees, hundreds of feet into the air, where the sun was sparkling through ancient leaves.

Finally he turned to his father with a look that said, *"Can we?"*

Mr. Lambchop sighed deeply and then cleared his throat. "Get back in the van, everybody," he said. "This has gone far enough."

Lily and Stanley's faces fell.

But then his dad winked. "We need

to let Mrs. Lambchop, Arthur, and Stanley's friend Thomas know that they shouldn't worry. It seems we won't be joining them again for a few days, at least!"

3

Introducing the Escapist

When he and his father climbed out of the van at the Foxes' farmhouse a few hours later, Stanley was greeted by a big shaggy dog that bounded up, flattened him to the ground, and licked his face.

"Sequoia!" a voice called. "Heel!" The dog leaped off of Stanley and sat panting beside him.

A barefoot woman with curly blond

hair and a flowing, brightly colored
dress reached for Stanley's hand, helping
him up. "I'm Lily's mom, Amber," she
said, and turned toward Mr. Lambchop.
"And you must be Stanley's father."

"It's George," Stanley's dad replied.

"Well, I want to thank you both for being part of our little caper." She threw one arm around Dr. Fox and put her other hand on Lily's shoulder. "When our Lily sets her mind to something, she never gives up."

The Foxes led them up to the farmhouse. After Stanley's father had called Stanley's mom to check in, they joined Lily and her parents for dinner around a worn wooden table. There were so many different colors of food, they reminded Stanley of the fruit and vegetable section of the supermarket.

"We grew most of this here on the farm," said Amber, serving Stanley some kale slaw. "In fact, if you eat fruits or vegetables back home that are grown in America, chances are they come from California. There's no place better on Earth." She rattled off the things on the table: "Artichokes, arugula, asparagus, avocados, basil, beets, broccoli, cantaloupe,

carrots, celery, corn, cucumbers, edamame, eggplant, escarole—"

"Mom," Lily gently interrupted. "They get the idea."

"But I'm only at the letter *e*!" complained her mother.

Stanley realized that Amber had been listing foods alphabetically, and he slapped his forehead.

"That's something *my* mom would do! She's crazy about anything which has to do with language."

Amber said, "I think you mean *that*, not *which*, Stanley."

Stanley and his father both laughed at how much she sounded like Mrs. Lambchop.

"I don't know which my mom likes more, vegetables or vowels," said Lily. "Last summer she attached a plow to the back of my wheelchair so I could help in the fields."

Stanley's father said, "A human plow, huh? I suppose that's how you got so strong, Lily."

Lily said, "I was born strong."

* * *

After a dessert of fresh blackberries, blueberries, and boysenberries with cream, Dr. Fox said, "Ready to head out to the barn?"

"I could've skipped dinner, I'm so ready," said Lily.

Following them to the big barn, Stanley was surprised to find there were no animals. Instead the inside of the barn looked like a spotless, high-tech body shop for fixing up cars—only without the cars. On the wall hung at least a dozen different wheelchairs gleaming like jewels. One looked more like a tiny Formula One racecar, red and white and shiny with a pointed

nose. One was clad in a varsity athlete's uniform, complete with white striped wheels instead of socks. One balanced on what looked like a pair of ice-skating blades instead of wheels, and it hung near a hockey stick with a sawed-off handle. And one looked like the bottom half of a ball gown, with sparkly fabric covering everything but the bottom of the wheels.

"What kind of a doctor *are* you, anyway?" Stanley's father asked.

"I have a PhD in mechanical engineering," replied Dr. Fox.

"And you *made* all these?" said Stanley.

"Lily and I designed and built them

together," said Dr. Fox.

"Which is your favorite?" Stanley asked Lily.

"Depends on the situation." She pointed to one that had paddles instead of wheels, and a strange mask sitting on the seat. "The first time I used my scuba chair was pretty awesome."

Lily rolled along, stopping in front of the last wheelchair in the bottom row: a sleek little black number.

"This," said Lily, "is the Escapist. She's the lightest wheelchair ever built, weighing in at less than eight pounds. She has fourteen hidden compartments. Each of her wheel spokes is a different

kind of tool: mini crowbar. Lockpick.
Radio antenna. She's what we're riding
out of Alcatraz."

"Speaking of Alcatraz," said Dr. Fox
as he spread a blueprint of the prison out
on a table. The four of them gathered
around it.

"So, you really think you can escape?" Stanley said. "What's the plan?"

"The only way in or out of the Rock is by ferry," Lily said. "So we'll take the ferry there from Fisherman's Wharf, just like any other tourists. The prison is a museum now, and we'll buy tickets for the last tour of the day. We'll hang at the back of the group until we come to the cell where the gangster Al 'Scarface' Capone used to live."

Dr. Fox took over. "You and Lily will enter the cell and close the door, locking yourselves inside. You will hide there until the museum closes and the lights in the cellblock go out."

"I'll pick the lock of the cell door," Lily continued. "Stanley, it's going to be your job to slip between bars and check under doors to make sure the coast is clear. There will be at least one night guard on duty, maybe more. We'll make our way along this hallway." Lily's finger traced a path through the prison. "Then we have to exit through this door to the outside without setting off any alarms. The final stage of the plan—crossing the Bay—will unfold on live TV."

"How are you going to get on TV if this is all a secret?" asked Stanley's father.

"Let's just say we know someone

in show business," Dr. Fox answered quickly.

"Once we get to this point," continued Lily, "we just have to cross the Bay to the other side. It's simple."

"Simple?" repeated Stanley. "What about the shark-infested waters?!"

Lily rolled her eyes. "They're really small sharks. Besides, you'll be pulling me pretty fast by that point."

"I can't swim that far!" Stanley protested.

"Why swim," Lily said, raising an eyebrow, "when a guy like you can fly?"

Stanley wrinkled his flat forehead. "Huh?"

But then he noticed his father nodding slowly. "You want Stanley to be your kite," he said quietly.

Lilly nodded excitedly. *"Exactly."*

Finally Stanley understood. He'd rise in the air, Lily would hold on to a string attached to him, and he'd pull her across the water.

"It won't work," he said with a shake of his head. "Even if the wind was strong enough, I can't pull that kind of weight."

"We've thought of that," said Dr. Fox. "That's why we're taking you to Silicon Valley first thing tomorrow."

Silicon Valley

"It's the technology capital of America, and maybe even the world. Silicon Valley is where computers were *born*," Lily explained to Stanley the next morning. They were riding in the back of the van while their fathers rode up front. "Dad's best friend owns a company there. He has a whole team of people helping us."

Stanley caught himself staring at Lily's feet. "Can I ask you something?" he said hesitantly.

"Shoot," said Lily.

"What happened to your legs?" he asked. "Sorry," he added quickly.

"You don't need to be embarrassed about asking." She shrugged. "I was born this way. I can't walk because my legs and my brain don't talk to each other very well."

"Do you ever wish you could walk?"

Lily smirked. "Do you ever wish you weren't flat?"

"Sometimes," admitted Stanley. "But

I don't really think about it that much anymore. It's just . . . the way I am."

Lily smiled. *"Exactly,"* she said.

Stanley was expecting an office building like the one where his father worked. But when they arrived, he found a campus that reminded him more of the University of Texas at Austin, where he had recently visited his friend Eduardo. People were playing Frisbee on a sprawling lawn surrounded by glass buildings.

They made their way to the biggest building, where Dr. Fox led them through a room filled with people at desks, Ping-Pong tables, and pinball

machines. A handful of employees in T-shirts were arguing and scrawling diagrams with Magic Markers on one wall.

Stanley's father murmured, "I wish *I* worked in a place like this."

"I wish we *lived* in a place like this," Stanley said.

They came to a desk in the middle of the floor, where a man with a beard was staring intently at something on his computer screen. He sat on a giant inflatable ball. When he looked up and saw Dr. Fox, his face broke into a huge smile.

"Theo!" he cried, grabbing his old friend in a bear hug. Then he saw Lily and said, "Lily pad!"

"Hiya, Uncle Jerry!" said Lily, rolling over for a squeeze.

"Jerry," said Dr. Fox, "I want you to meet Stanley Lambchop and his father, George."

"We've been waiting for you!" said Uncle Jerry, pumping Stanley's hand. "Everyone's been working around the clock." He ushered them down the hall to a bank of elevators. Inside, Jerry punched *B* for basement. "Wait until you see what we've come up with!"

The elevator doors opened onto a laboratory. People in white coats and sneakers were hurrying back and forth, but they all stopped in their tracks when they saw Stanley and Lily.

"Team!" said Uncle Jerry. "Meet Stanley!"

Everyone called out welcoming words.

"Stanley's just like us," he said. "He thinks Lily Pad here has a crazy idea. But you know the thing about crazy ideas? They're the only ones big enough to change the world. That's why he's agreed to be part of her plan. So let's do *our* part and give Stanley a boost, shall we?"

Uncle Jerry pressed a button, and a big black screen rose up from a slot in the floor. In front of it hung a glimmering black jumpsuit stretched around a mannequin shaped just like Stanley. The suit covered everything except the eyes, like a ninja costume. Meanwhile, there was webbed fabric connecting the arms to the sides of the

legs, almost like the wings of a bat.

"Coooool," said Stanley.

"Introducing the Flat Stanley Flight Suit Version 8.2," announced Uncle Jerry. "Strong as steel. Waterproof. Lightning-proof. Windproof. Tear-proof. Injury-resistant. Stanley, I think it's safe to say you're in for the smoothest flight of your life. But that's not all." He pushed another button, and the big screen behind the suit turned bright green. All at once, the suit turned the same shade of green. The board turned blue, and the suit turned blue. Stanley could barely see it against the background. "It's also self-camouflaging," Uncle Jerry said excitedly.

"Stanley the Flat Chameleon!" Lily giggled as she spun around in her chair. "As far as the world knows, I'll just be a girl in a wheelchair rolling across the water . . . like *magic*."

Stanley couldn't believe his eyes: his very own superhero suit! "My brother, Arthur, is going to f-freak out!" he stammered.

Uncle Jerry and his team cheered.

"Now there's only one last puzzle piece we need," Dr. Fox said, throwing an arm around both Stanley and his father. "Next stop, Hollywood."

"Why Hollywood?" asked Stanley's father.

Stanley couldn't get any more excited. He'd always wanted to go to Hollywood!

Lily rubbed her hands together. "Because that's where our man in show business is."

5

Hollywood, Here We Come

"I still don't understand," Stanley's father said as they huddled in the back of the van outside the gates of the movie studio. "Why do we have to sneak onto a movie set if we're visiting someone you know?"

"Because," Lily answered with a roll of her eyes, "it's a *surprise*."

"Okay," said Dr. Fox, pressing a

fake mustache onto his upper lip. "Everybody know their roles?"

Stanley adjusted his mirrored sunglasses. His father straightened the scarf around his neck. And Lily punched a leather-gloved fist into her other palm. They rolled out of the back of the van.

Stanley couldn't help gaping up at the palm trees that lined the sidewalk. As they approached the security booth at the edge of the studio lot, a guard stepped out.

"I have the famous Flat Stanley Lambchop here to visit the set of *Storm Warriors*!" announced Stanley's father in a brassy voice. With his business suit

and a scarf around his neck, he looked like a real movie mogul.

"Is he on the list?" said the guard.

"The list?" shouted Mr. Lambchop. "My client is the most famous flat kid in the world, and you want to know if he's on the list?"

"All right, all right," said the security guard, throwing up his hands. "But what about the rest of you?"

"I'm a big agent, mister!" boomed Mr. Lambchop. "I can't wait to tell your boss you don't know who I am!"

Stanley bit his lip to keep from laughing.

"And I am Stanley's trainer," said Dr. Fox in a Russian accent. He was wearing a red tracksuit. His mustache was coming up on one side. "Flat muscles need good exercise."

The guard peered down at Lily. She flexed her fists slowly. "I'm da bodyguard," she grunted.

The guard rolled his eyes and waved the four of them through.

"It worked!" whispered Lily. "Now all we have to do is find the set of *Storm Warriors*!"

"Who are we looking for, anyway?" whispered Stanley, running to keep up.

"You'll see," said Lily.

They turned a corner.

"There it is!" whispered Dr. Fox, pointing to a placard that read STORM

WARRIORS beside the entrance to a big warehouse-like building.

Mr. Lambchop tried the huge sliding door, but it wouldn't budge. Then Dr. Fox tried. Finally Lily pursed her lips and grabbed the handle, pulling with all her might. The door squeaked open an inch, but that was it.

"I can fit," Stanley whispered. "I'll check things out and report back. Wait here." He paused. "Whom should I ask for?"

Dr. Fox said, "You'll know him when you see him."

Stanley said, "But who—"

Lily held up her hands. "Trust us," she said.

Stanley sighed, handed his sunglasses to Lily, and slipped inside. It was very dark. He crept forward.

"This is the big one, everybody," a voice announced over a loudspeaker. "Remember, nothing loose on set. Everything tied down? Good. Cue rain."

It started pouring. Stanley curled his head down to keep his face dry. *How do they make it rain from the ceiling like that?* he thought.

"Lightning and thunder," boomed the voice.

The room flashed, and a deafening crash shook Stanley's whole body.

"And . . . cue tornado!"

A powerful swirl of wind suddenly seized the room, and Stanley was pulled into the air. "Whoa!" he yelled.

A segment of picket fence came flying toward him, and Stanley narrowly slipped through its panels. He dodged a fake cow. A couch came up behind him, forcing him to sit.

Riding through the air on the couch, Stanley saw two men facing off over the spinning center of the tornado! They flipped through the air at each other. One landed a kick in the other's chest, sending his opponent flying . . . right onto the couch beside Stanley.

"Stanley-san?" said the stricken warrior in disbelief.

"CUT!" the loudspeaker voice cried.

The wind instantly died and so did the rain, thunder, and lightning. Stanley was surprised to find that the couch was actually suspended at the top of a crane. On another crane across the set was the car Stanley had narrowly avoided. And sitting beside him was his old friend, the Japanese movie star Oda Nobu.

"WHAT IS THAT KID-SHAPED SIGN DOING FLYING AROUND ON SET!" the director's voice shouted.

"Stanley-san," said Oda Nobu as the crane descended to the ground. "What are you doing here?"

"I was . . . I am . . ." Stanley sputtered.

His mind was reeling. *Did Lily know Oda Nobu was here?* he thought. *Is Oda Nobu our connection in show business?*

"Can you come with me?" Stanley gestured for his old friend to follow. At the giant door, he stepped aside and let Oda Nobu pull it open.

Lily rolled right in, almost barreling over Oda Nobu. She stuck out a hand. "It's a real pleasure to meet you, Mr. Nobu! I'm a big fan. Stanley's always talking about you, and we thought we'd bring him down here to say hi. Plus, I knew you were just the man to help us with our plan to change the world!"

Stanley couldn't help but laugh. *Lily is fearless!* he thought.

"Any friend of Stanley's is a friend of mine," said Oda Nobu. "What is this plan of yours?"

Lily peered around to make sure no

one was listening. "We'd like you to hold a live news conference to bring the world's attention to a daring escape from Alcatraz."

"But who would attempt such an escape?" said Oda Nobu.

Lily sat up straighter. "You're looking at her!"

Hitting the Beach

Less than twenty-four hours remained until the escape. There was only one thing left to do: practice.

Oda Nobu, Stanley, and Lily huddled in the back of the Fox family's van as it raced up Highway 1, along the Pacific coast from Los Angeles toward San Francisco. On one wall of the van hung the blueprint of Alcatraz.

Stanley practiced slipping his head through the slit in the partition to the front seat without Dr. Fox and his father noticing. Lily picked a lock while wearing a blindfold. Oda Nobu went over his script: His agent had informed the networks that both he and his wife, the famed matador Carmen del Junco, would be appearing at Fisherman's Wharf in San Francisco to make a "shocking announcement" at exactly 7:15 tomorrow evening. The press was already aflutter with rumors that the international celebrity couple might be breaking up.

Suddenly the van stopped. Dr. Fox opened the back doors, and sunlight streamed in. Stanley heard the crashing of waves. A sign pointing back in the direction they came read SANTA BARBARA.

"The beach here is deserted," Dr. Fox announced. "Stanley, Lily, it's time for a test flight."

Once Stanley squeezed into his flight suit, Oda Nobu looked at him admiringly. "That is the finest ninja suit I have ever seen."

Stanley puffed out his chest. "Nice, huh?"

Stanley sat on the sand while Dr. Fox fiddled with the extra-fine wires that would attach him to the Escapist—also known as the wheelchair Lily was using

for her stunt. His suit turned light beige to match the sand. Oda Nobu gasped and announced that he must have one. "Also," he added, "Carmen could use such a suit for her bullfights. She would be invincible!" Stanley grinned at the thought of bullfighting with Carmen, as he had in Mexico.

Finally they were ready. Stanley's father said, "Stanley, I want you to be careful. Lily's safety is in your hands."

Stanley nodded nervously. He hadn't thought of it that way before, and it made him nervous. After all, it wasn't so long ago that he'd been terrified of the wind while driving through a wind farm in Texas.

But then, too, he had put fear aside to help his friends.

Now it was time to help Lily.

Up ahead, she slowly rolled to the edge of the water, and Stanley followed. Before them, a giant wave crested and crashed. The white foam licked Stanley's feet and the bottom of the Escapist's wheels.

"Lily," said Stanley, "you're going to have to throw me really hard to get me up in the air. It has to be like when my little brother, Arthur, threw me in Australia. Like you're throwing a boomerang."

Lily took his hands. "Stanley," she said, taking a deep breath, "let's blow

this taco stand." And she heaved him into the air with all her might.

Stanley spread out his arms, and the wind found him at once. It was as if he'd been hit by a rocket. "Whoa!" he cried, bursting through one wisp of cloud, and then another. Suddenly he stopped rising and leveled out.

His suit shimmered pale blue. Stanley felt a small tug on his wires and heard a triumphant squeal from below.

Stanley looked down. It took him a moment to make them out, but there they were: two tracks of white carving a path through the water. They were the wake created by Lily's wheels, skimming the surface. He tilted slightly, and the white trails began etching out a circle.

Lily Fox was kitesurfing, and Stanley was her kite.

The Great Escape

The next day, Oda Nobu saw Lily, Stanley, and their fathers off on the last ferry to Alcatraz. Nearby, reporters were already beginning to gather for Oda and Carmen's "surprise" news conference.

It was late in the afternoon, and the Bay was choppy. Stanley's edges fluttered in the wind, and his father held his hand to make sure he didn't blow away. The red, ghostly outline of the Golden Gate Bridge rose behind them as the ferry plowed toward Alcatraz.

It was less than two miles to the island, but Stanley thought the distance felt much too great for anyone to cross without a boat.

Inside the prison, they hung at the back of the group as the tour guide explained how Alcatraz was first used as a prison during the Civil War. But Stanley was too nervous to pay close attention.

Lily wore all black. Meanwhile, Stanley was wearing his flight suit beneath his clothes. Sweating, he passed mug shot after mug shot of hardened criminals who had served time on the Rock. Stanley imagined what they might say: *We never escaped. You won't either.*

Finally they arrived at the cellblock that Stanley remembered from the

blueprint. It was long, narrow, and
lined with cells on both sides. Each tiny,
broken-down cell contained nothing
more than a toilet, a sink, and a small
cot.

And then here it was: the cell in which America's most notorious gangster, Al "Scarface" Capone, had done his time. The door was open for visitors, just as they expected.

As the guide spoke about Capone's years at Alcatraz, Stanley's father pulled him close and whispered "Good luck." Dr. Fox kept his eyes on the guide and then gave the hand signal: The guide was looking away. Stanley shimmied out of his baggy clothes and slipped into the cell, wearing nothing but his flight suit. He leaned his body against a back corner, his suit turning pale yellow to match the wall. With a flick of the wrist, Lily backed in behind the screen formed by Stanley's camouflaged body.

Dr. Fox leaned against the cell door, gently shutting it. The door locked with a terrible click.

And then Lily and Stanley were alone.

Just when Stanley thought he couldn't wait a second longer, the lights went off, right on schedule. Alcatraz was locked down for the night. The cellblock was now lit only by the eerie red glow of emergency lights.

Stanley stood and crept to the cell door. In his black, self-camouflaging flight suit, he could barely see his own body in the darkness. He twisted sideways, inserting his head between the bars, and looked up and down the cellblock.

"All clear," he whispered to Lily. Lily reached down and pulled a spoke from her wheel: the lockpick. She rolled up against the bars, reaching around with 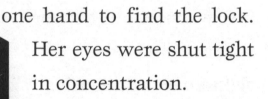 one hand to find the lock. Her eyes were shut tight in concentration.

There was a loud click, and the door swung open with a painful squeal.

Stanley and Lily froze. After a count of ten, he followed her out of the cell.

Lily rolled through the deserted prison. Stanley crept ahead of her, peeking around corners. He gave a signal when the coast was clear.

They were inching along the eastern cellblock when Stanley saw a ray of light down the hall. He held a hand up to Lily, and she rolled to a stop.

They heard footsteps, and a short, heavy guard with a flashlight turned a corner. He was coming their way!

Stanley spotted a blanket on a cot in an empty cell. He darted between the bars, grabbed the blanket, and threw it over Lily. Then he threw himself on top of her and tucked his face out of sight.

The guard's footsteps slowed, and he

ran his
beam over them.

"Now, who left this
chair here?" he murmured
to himself. Stanley heard the guard's
heavy footsteps come closer.

"Well, I might as well rest my weary
bones," the guard said with a sigh.

Oh no, thought Stanley. *He's going to
sit on us!*

Stanley and Lily braced for impact. But just then, the big guard's walkie-talkie crackled to life. "Barney, where are you? Aren't you done with your rounds yet?"

Barney grunted and straightened up. "Yeah, yeah," he said to himself. "I'm coming." He ambled down the hall, grumbling as he went.

When Stanley could no longer hear the guard's footsteps, he leaped up, threw off the blanket, and turned to give Lily a look of relief. But she was already on the move. He ran to keep up.

Finally they arrived at the heavy door that would lead them out of the prison, to the outside. It was kept shut by a rusty old lock.

Lily silently pulled another spoke from the Escapist's wheel: the crowbar. She stuck it in the side of the door, and gave a quick push. The lock broke with a crack.

"Check the other side," whispered Lily. "If the coast is clear, we'll make a break for it."

Stanley slipped under the bottom of the door, and the salty night air struck him in the face. All was quiet in the deserted grounds of the prison, and the waters of San Francisco Bay lapped onto the shore far down below. He stood up outside and stretched his arms.

With a flourish, Stanley opened

the door for his partner—and an earsplitting siren pierced the air.

He'd tripped the alarm!

"Come on!" Lily barreled forward, scooping Stanley onto her lap. A spotlight flicked on somewhere above them. Lily weaved the wheelchair just out of its reach.

Stanley suddenly saw that they were surrounded by a barbed wire fence that cut them off from the shoreline. *That wasn't on the blueprint!* he realized.

"Prepare for emergency takeoff!" said Lily.

"We're too far from shore!" screamed Stanley over the sirens. "If you launch me from here, your wheelchair will never clear that fence!"

"PREPARE FOR EMERGENCY TAKEOFF!" repeated Lily fiercely, turning the wheelchair on a dime as the spotlight's glare grazed her elbow.

Still on Lily's lap, Stanley quickly connected the wires attaching him to the Escapist. Lily backed away from the fence, and the spotlight caught them. "DO NOT FLEE!" a voice commanded over a loudspeaker.

Lily took Stanley's hands and looked him squarely in the eye.

"Let's blow this taco stand," she said through gritted teeth.

And she threw Stanley over the fence and right off the edge of the Rock.

Sky High

Stanley kept his eyes trained on Lily as her wheelchair lifted off. They climbed swiftly, but then he felt a terrible lurch—the wheels of the Escapist had snagged the barbed wire at the top of the fence.

"Lily!" screamed Stanley. No matter how hard the wind pulled, it couldn't blow them free. The force against

Stanley was so great, he could barely breathe. Caught like a bug in the spotlight, Lily took a spoke from the Escapist's wheel, and pulled it apart into two handles. They were wire cutters! Lily was snipping the barbed wire!

All at once, the Escapist was free, and Stanley blew out over the bay. Almost immediately, he felt a series of hard, jagged tugs on the wires that ran down to the wheelchair.

Lily must be bumping the rocks on her way to the water! thought Stanley. He angled upward, pulling her higher.

The San Francisco skyline twinkled up ahead, a slim pyramid-shaped

building leading the way. *She must be over the water by now,* thought Stanley, and he slowly descended until he felt a smooth bump in the lines. Lily's wheelchair was skimming the surface of San Francisco Bay.

Down below, a spotlight caught Lily in its circular halo. But it wasn't coming from Alcatraz. It was coming from across the bay, from Oda Nobu's press conference. The world was watching Lily speed along, miraculously rolling on the surface of the water. Doing the *impossible.*

Stanley was overcome by a wave of happiness. Then a faint sound filled his

ears: people cheering from the shore.
Lily was almost there!

Stanley got ready for the moment his
friend would detach the wires, rolling
onto the shore without anyone knowing
how she'd crossed the bay. He felt a

slight jerk as the line was released, and he let himself safely descend, floating down like he'd learned to do at the wind farm in Texas.

Stanley fluttered on top of a building overlooking the press conference. Below, TV cameras were swarming around Lily. From the stage, his friend Oda Nobu said, "Ladies and gentlemen, I give you Lily Fox, the first person in history to escape from Alcatraz!"

The crowd went wild. Lily beamed.

"Thank you! Thank you all!" she shouted into the microphone. "I couldn't have done it alone! I had someone special looking down on me!" She scanned the rooftops, her eyes

twinkling. And Stanley, invisible in his suit, took an invisible bow.

Two hours later, Stanley was out for a crab dinner on Fisherman's Wharf with his parents; his brother, Arthur; and his friend Thomas Anthony Jeffrey.

"What do you mean you won't tell us where you've been for the last three days?" cried Arthur.

"It's a secret," said Stanley.

"George, you said someone needed Stanley's help," said Stanley's mother. "Who was it?"

"I can't say," said Stanley's father.

"Come on, Stanley," said Thomas. "Can't you tell us anything about this

latest adventure of yours?"

Stanley looked down at his cracked crab. He felt bad. "I'll let you try on my superhero suit," he offered.

"You got a superhero suit?" cried

Arthur. "How come I can't have a superhero suit?"

Suddenly a murmur swept through the restaurant. Everyone was turning to look. And then Stanley saw them: Lily and her parents had arrived, right on schedule. They rolled right up to the Lambchops' table.

Lily gave Stanley a triumphant high five.

"You're the girl who escaped from Alcatraz!" Stanley's mother exclaimed.

"May I have your autograph?" Thomas asked.

"Everyone, this is my friend Lily," said Stanley, "and these are her parents. You all want to know about my

adventure? Well, it's not my adventure to share. It's hers."

"Hi, everybody," said Lily. "Thanks for lending me Stanley and Mr. Lambchop." She paused, and Stanley was surprised to see that she was blushing. Then she took a deep breath and began. "It started with a dream. And the trick with any dream is figuring out how to make it real."

When the Lambchops finally returned home the next day, Stanley was awfully happy to see his and Arthur's room. Somehow, of all his adventures, this one seemed like the biggest journey.

Stanley studied his bulletin board. There he had souvenirs from his travels: a newspaper article about how Stanley saved Mount Rushmore, a photo of him bullfighting in Mexico, and on and on. He rummaged through the front of his bag and pulled out the front page of this morning's *California Chronicle*: "Daredevil Escapes Alcatraz Without Getting Wet." In the photo was Lily, beaming. Stanley, of course, was nowhere to be seen.

And, as he tacked the clipping to his bulletin board, Stanley realized that this was the souvenir that made him proudest of all.

WHAT YOU NEED TO KNOW ABOUT ALCATRAZ AND SAN FRANCISCO

The word *alcatraz* means "strange bird" or pelican. The island "de los alcatraces" was named by Spanish explorer Lt. Juan Manuel de Ayala in 1775.

Al Capone played the banjo in the Alcatraz prison band, the Rock Islanders, which gave concerts for other inmates.

Thirty-six inmates put the "escape-proof" Alcatraz to the test. But there were no confirmed prisoner escapes from Alcatraz.

Alcatraz was home to the Pacific Coast's first lighthouse, activated in 1854.

In 1849, San Francisco's harbor was filled with abandoned ships. The crews had deserted the ships to head inland for the gold fields.

The Golden Gate Bridge was not supposed to be red. The steel beams used to build the bridge were coated in a red-and-orange color to protect it from corrosive elements.

The night before the 1906 earthquake, world-famous Italian opera singer Enrico Caruso performed in San Francisco.

President Millard Fillmore made Alcatraz a military fortress in 1850.

When the Golden Gate Bridge was finished in May 1937, Chief Engineer Joseph B. Strauss wrote a poem called "The Mighty Task is Done."

The cable car is a national historic monument, the only one in the world that moves! It was built in 1873 and today transports 9.7 million people around the city each year.

In 1914, Makoto Hagiwara made the first fortune cookie in San Francisco. He was a Japanese immigrant and the designer of Golden Gate Park's famous Japanese Tea Garden.

San Francisco has some weird laws: it is illegal to clean your rug by beating it outside, to walk an elephant down Market Street without a leash, and to wipe your windshield using your underwear.

Denim jeans were invented in San Francisco for Gold Rush miners in California. The denim was tough enough to last and protect their skin.

James Marshall found gold at Sutter's Mill in 1848. His discovery caused many immigrants to come into the city to seek their fortune.

Irish coffee was first invented in San Francisco. And there are now more than 300 coffee shops in San Francisco.

There's No Place on Earth
That a Flat Kid Can't Go!

Don't Miss the First Worldwide Adventure:

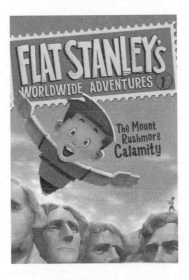

Turn the Page for a Sneak Peek!

Ready, Set...

"Sleeping bags?" George Lambchop called out to his wife, Harriet.

"Check!" answered Mrs. Lambchop.

"Wholesome snacks for the boys?"

"Check!" replied Mr. Lambchop.

The Lambchop family was preparing for their vacation to Mount Rushmore in the Black Hills of South Dakota.

They were each very excited about the adventure.

Mr. Lambchop was excited because he was going to collect another state park sticker for the rear window of the car.

Mrs. Lambchop was excited because she was going to learn more about the history of South Dakota.

Their younger son, Arthur, was excited because he was hoping to meet some real, live cowboys.

And Stanley, the Lambchops' older son, was excited because he was going somewhere nobody would recognize him.

Not long ago, Stanley had awakened

to find that his enormous bulletin board had fallen upon him during the night. Since then, the family had gotten used to having a flattened boy in the house. But when he ventured outside, he often caused a commotion: "Look, Marge! There he is . . . the famous flattened kid! Wonder what new adventure he's up to now?" Or, "Say there, Flatty, mind if we take a picture?"

The truth is, both Lambchop brothers were getting a bit tired of all the attention Stanley was getting. It would be nice, they agreed, to get away someplace where people didn't make such a fuss.

"Well, I think we're ready," said Mr.

Lambchop, surveying the mountain of suitcases and camping equipment in the hall.

"Not quite, dear," replied Mrs. Lambchop. "Remember, we still have to consult Dr. Dan about Stanley's travel needs. Better safe than sorry."

"Well, the boy is still flat," Doctor Dan pronounced, when he was finished with his examination.

"Yes, we know that," said Stanley's father. "We were wondering whether such a trip would be suitable for Stanley in his present condition. Mount Rushmore's elevation is 5,725 feet, for one thing. And we'll be traveling by automobile along the scenic highways at a fairly high velocity."

Here Mrs. Lambchop interrupted her husband with a chuckle. "Not too high a velocity, of course," she said.

Mr. Lambchop smiled at his wife's joke. Both she and Mr. Lambchop were always careful to obey local speed limits. "Still," he said, "we did feel it would be wise to check with you."

"It's a good thing you did. More people

should be concerned about the effects of travel on the body. The human being is a very complex organism. Even we doctors, with our extensive knowledge, don't completely understand it."

"Oh, dear," Mrs. Lambchop said anxiously. "Will it be all right for Stanley to come with us?"

"Of course!" said Doctor Dan. "I can't think of any reason why not!"

GO!

The next day, after a hearty breakfast, the Lambchop family began to pack the car for their big trip. In went the tent, four sleeping bags, and the rest of the camping gear. In went the suitcases, the cameras, and coolers. Arthur came out with his arms full—his authentic cowboy saddle, his authentic cowboy harmonica, and his authentic cowboy lasso.

"Oh, dear," Mrs. Lambchop murmured, surveying the overstuffed car. "There doesn't seem to be much room for the boys!"

"Playing cowboys is for little kids," Stanley said. "Now that I've been in the newspaper, I'm too grown-up for that sort of thing. I think Arthur should leave all that stuff behind."

Arthur glared at his brother. "Stanley can ride on the roof," he suggested.

Mr. Lambchop considered this. "Well, if we lash him down securely . . ."

"I think not," decided Mrs. Lambchop. "We will be pointing out many sights along the way. I don't want Stanley to miss them."

And so both boys squeezed into the backseat with much grumbling, and the family set out.

Along the way, the Lambchops did indeed come upon many wondrous sights: inspiring cityscapes, fields of bountiful crops, and numerous glories of nature.

"We should all be grateful to have good eyesight as we travel through this great land of ours," Mr. Lambchop noted. The rest of the Lambchops agreed they were very fortunate indeed.

Every time they crossed into a new state, the family recited its motto and sang its song. They played License Plate Bingo and I Spy, and the hours passed fairly quickly. Nonetheless, everyone was delighted to arrive at the gates of Mount Rushmore State Park. The boys craned their heads out the windows to gaze up at the sixty-foot-tall faces carved in the mountain, while Mr. Lambchop paid the admission fees. And as soon as the car was parked, they sprang out.

"I'm all crumpled!" Stanley groused, trying to smooth himself out.

"Well, I'm practically flattened!" complained Arthur.

"Boys, hurry along," said Mrs. Lambchop. "We're just in time to catch the last tour group."

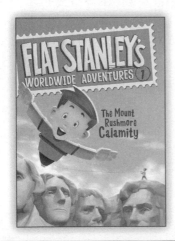

J

(Flat Stanley's worldwide
 adventures ; #12)